A TRUMPET CLUB SPECIAL EDITION

To Susan Korn Blutter and William James Gray

Published by The Trumpet Club
a division of Bantam Doubleday Dell Publishing Group, Inc.
666 Fifth Avenue, New York, New York 10103

ISBN: 0-440-84340-5

This edition published by arrangement with Viking Penguin, a division of Penguin Books USA Inc.
Set in Aster
Printed in the United States of America
September 1990

10 9 8 7 6 5 4 3 2 1
UPC

Spud Jenkins and Joe Turner
were a couple of real cut-ups.

They made their mothers old
before their time.

To say nothing of Spud's
little brother, Jerome.

Being a cut-up was a full time job.

It required imagination...

and considerable skill.

"They ought to be locked up," folks said.

If it wasn't one thing
it was another.

"It's too late to separate them" said Spud's mom.

"School starts soon," said Joe's mom.

"Maybe we can hold out."

One afternoon the cut-ups
were relaxing between activities.
"We get away with murder," said Spud.
"That's because we're so smart," said Joe.

"Hello, boys," said a young lady.

Her name was Mary Frances,

and she drove her own sports car.

"Wow!" said Spud and Joe.

"What a great car!"

They fell all over themselves
trying to make a nice impression.

"You guys are real cut-ups," said Mary Frances.
"Where'd you get that car?" said Joe.

"I built it myself," said Mary Frances.

"Oh, go on," they said.

"I *did,*" said Mary Frances.

"And I built a rocket ship too."

"Sure, sure," they said.

"I'll show you," said Mary Frances. "Hop in."

And she took them over to Maple Street.

Mary
Frances

"Who lives there?" said Joe.
"Oh, that's where dear Mr. Spurgle lives,"
said Mary Frances.
"Look at all those signs!" said Spud.
"Those are just for grown-ups,"
said Mary Frances.
"Dear Mr. Spurgle lets me play
in his yard whenever I want.
He just loves kids.
He used to be an assistant principal."

PRIVATE PROPERTY
KEEP OFF!!
NO!
YOU'LL BE SORRY
DON'T YOU DARE!
I SHOW NO MERCY

At that moment Lamar J. Spurgle,
who'd had enough of kids to last him a lifetime,
was observing them through
his high-powered binoculars.
"There's that brat Mary Frances Hooley," he said.
"And two of her little friends.
If that kid's car so much as touches my yard,
I'll grab it and keep it."
Lamar J. Spurgle had a whole room
full of kids' stuff.

Mary Frances hurried them on by
and took them to her backyard.
"Wow!" said Spud. "You weren't kidding!"
"Does it fly?" said Joe.
"Of course it flies," said Mary Frances.
"I don't fly it myself because I get nosebleeds."
"Let us, let us!" cried Spud and Joe.
"Well, I don't know..." said Mary Frances.
"*Please!*" they cried.

Mary Frances finally agreed
to let the cut-ups make a test flight.
"Hot dog!" cried Spud and Joe.
And they climbed aboard.
"Are you ready?" said Mary Frances.
"We're ready!" said the cut-ups.
Mary Frances released the giant spring.
And the rocket zoomed into the air.

Over the bushes it flew,

right past Lamar J. Spurgle's window,

and smack into his prized flower bed.

“My zinnias!” cried Spurgle.

Out of the house he charged.
"You'll pay for this!" he cried.
"Holy smoke!" cried Spud.
"Run for your life!"

The cut-ups tore off down Maple Street.
But Lamar J. Spurgle was gaining fast.
"We're done for!" cried Spud.
"Got you now!" cried Spurgle.

Mary Frances rushed into Spurgle's house
and gathered up as much stuff as she could carry.
"Thanks, boys," she said.

And she laughed all the way home.

Just as Spurgle was about to pounce
his battery went dead
and the cut-ups were able to make a safe getaway.

"I never forget a face!" called out Spurgle.

"Gosh," said Joe. "That was a close call.
I guess Mary Frances was wrong
about that guy."
"Let's forget the whole thing," said Spud.
"School starts soon
and we can really cut loose."

But little did they know...

That Lamar J. Spurgle had decided
to return to education.
And Lamar J. Spurgle never forgot a face.